Dear Parents and Educators,

Welcome to Penguin Young Readers! As parents and educators, you know that each child develops at his or her own pace—in terms of speech, critical thinking, and, of course, reading. Penguin Young Readers recognizes this fact. As a result, each Penguin Young Readers book is assigned a traditional easy-to-read level (1–4) as well as a Guided Reading Level (A–P). Both of these systems will help you choose the right book for your child. Please refer to the back of each book for specific leveling information. Penguin Young Readers features esteemed authors and illustrators, stories about favorite characters, fascinating nonfiction, and more!

Holiday Helper

LEVEL 2

GUIDED READING LEVEL **G**

This book is perfect for a **Progressing Reader** who:
- can figure out unknown words by using picture and context clues;
- can recognize beginning, middle, and ending sounds;
- can make and confirm predictions about what will happen in the text; and
- can distinguish between fiction and nonfiction.

Here are some **activities** you can do during and after reading this book:
- Problem/Solution: In this story, Scout wants to help her family with holiday celebrations. The problem is she keeps making messes. Discuss the solution to Scout's problem, and how she finally helps her family.
- Picture Clues: Often, pictures tell you something about the story that is not told in words. Have the child go back through and tell you the story by looking at only the pictures.

Remember, sharing the love of reading with a child is the best gift you can give!

—Bonnie Bader, EdM
  Penguin Young Readers program

*Penguin Young Readers are leveled by independent reviewers applying the standards developed by Irene Fountas and Gay Su Pinnell in *Matching Books to Readers: Using Leveled Books in Guided Reading*, Heinemann, 1999.

PENGUIN YOUNG READERS
Published by the Penguin Group
Penguin Group (USA) LLC, 375 Hudson Street, New York, New York 10014, USA

· USA | Canada | UK | Ireland | Australia | New Zealand | India | South Africa | China

penguin.com
A Penguin Random House Company

Text copyright © 2014 by Jill Abramson. Illustrations copyright © 2014 by Deborah Melmon.
All rights reserved. Published by Penguin Young Readers, an imprint of Penguin Group (USA) LLC,
345 Hudson Street, New York, New York 10014. Manufactured in China.

Library of Congress Cataloging-in-Publication Data is available.

ISBN 978-0-448-45677-5 (pbk)   10 9 8 7 6 5 4 3 2
ISBN 978-0-448-47780-0 (hc)   10 9 8 7 6 5 4 3 2 1

A Puppy Diaries BOOK

Holiday Helper

by Jill Abramson and Jane O'Connor
illustrated by Deborah Melmon

Penguin Young Readers
An Imprint of Penguin Group (USA) LLC

Hello.

My name is Scout.

And this is Baby.

Baby is my best friend.

We are both puppies.

Only I am a real puppy and

Baby isn't.

She always needs my help.

Today we are going outside to play.

It is cold.

I help Baby get dressed.

I put on her hat and coat.

We are ready to go.

Snow!

Oh no.

I will help fix this.

Look, look!

My family is home.

They have so many boxes.

I can help them.

Maybe we are having a party.

Look at all the food.

I can help cook.

Oh no.

What a mess!

I want to help clean up.

But it is late.

It is time to go to sleep.

I help Baby get into our bed.

I hear something!

Who is there?

Baby is scared.

I tell her it is okay.

I go to take a look.

Wow!

Red and green.

Blue and yellow.

Big and small.

Time to play!

Oh no.

What a mess!

I want to help clean up.

But I have to sit in my bed.

It is time to trim the tree.

Red and green.

Blue and yellow.

26

I see something is missing.

I am a good holiday helper.